Who Will Help Santa This Year?

Jerry Pallotta

Cartwheel BOOKS® SCHOLASTIC INC.

New York   Toronto   London   Auckland   Sydney
Mexico City   New Delhi   Hong Kong   Buenos Aires

David Biedrzycki

For elf Cindy and elf Mickey! – J. P.
Thank you, Ciro Giordano. – D. B.

ISBN-13: 978-0-545-01160-0
ISBN-10: 0-545-01160-4
Text copyright © 2006 by Jerry Pallotta.
Illustrations copyright © 2006 by David Biedrzycki.

10 9 8 7 6 5 4 3   8 9 10 11/0

Printed in Singapore   46
This edition first printing, October 2007

The job was too big! I couldn't make all the toys.

I had a workshop and plenty of great tools.

It was time to look for helpers.

I tried dragons.

Ah-ah-choo! The toys got cooked!

I tried fairies.

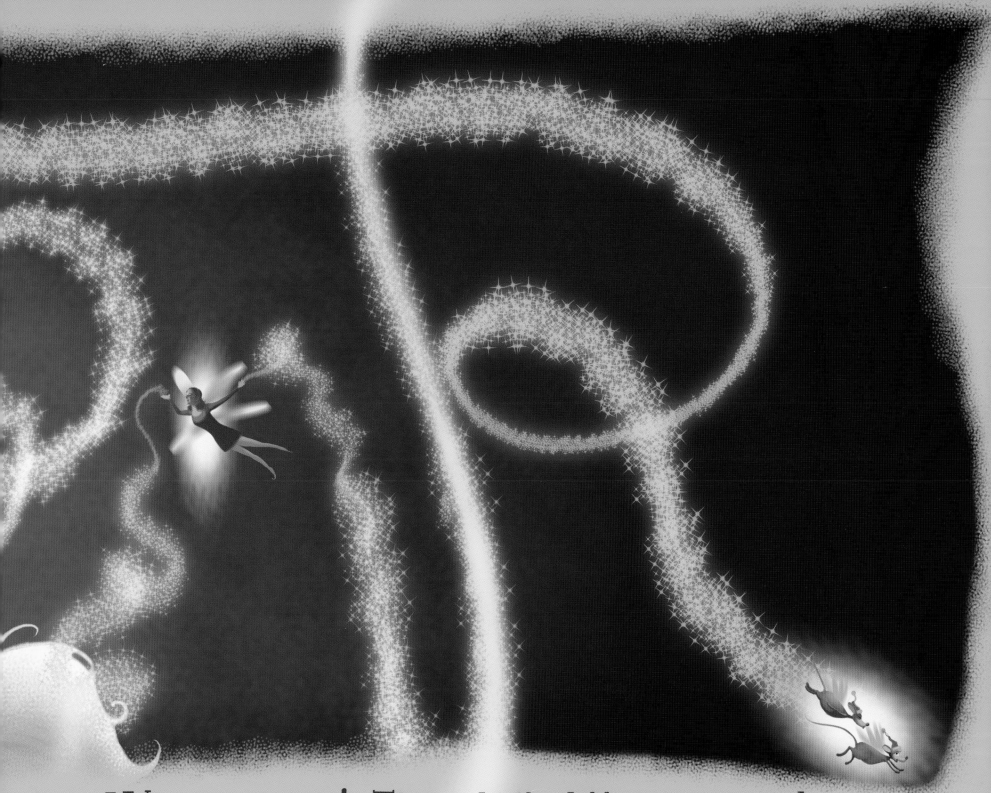

What a mess! They left glitter everywhere.

Bigfoot was a GIGANTIC mistake!

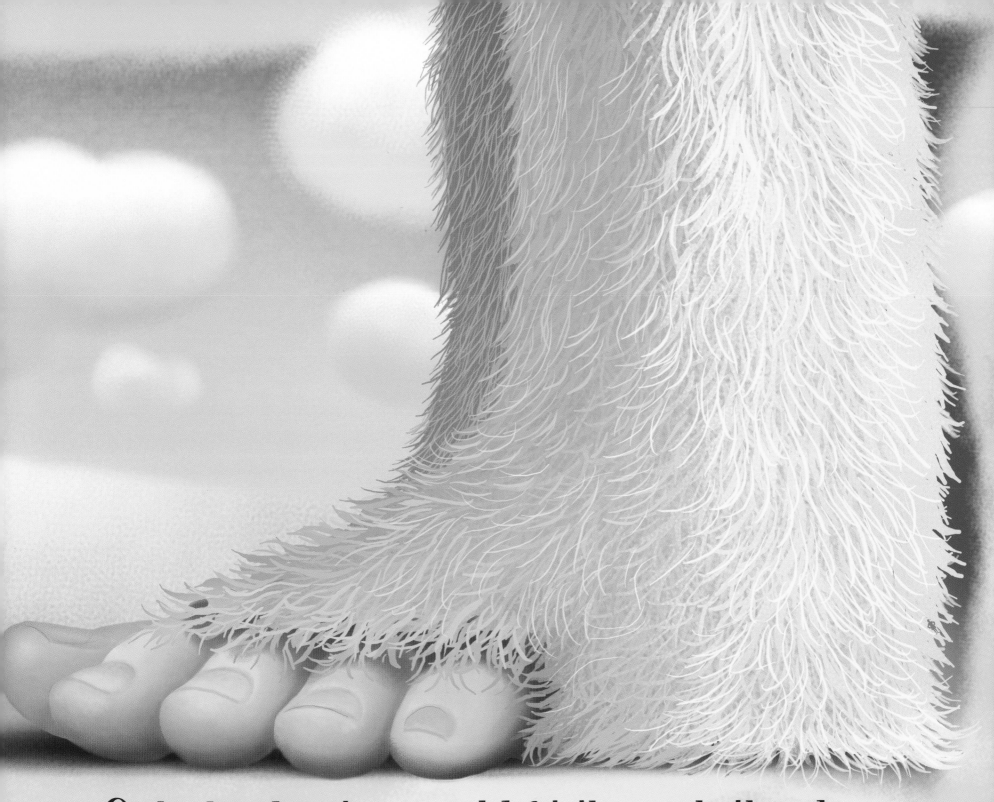

Only his big toe could fit through the door.

I tried mummies.

They were only good at wrapping.

I had good luck with leprechauns.

But they ran away to chase rainbows.

I tried garden gnomes.

"Hey! Kids like TOYS! Not brussels sprouts!"

I hired mermaids.

The fishing was good. Oh! No! The toys got soaked.

Aliens only made spaceships and funny noises.

Meep! Meep! And they never heard of Christmas.

I tried unicorns.

Uh-oh! Hooves! They couldn't hold the tools.

Wizards wanted to help.

Poof! They turned me into a frog!

Elves came looking for work. They had great advice.

"Kiss him! Kiss him! Kiss him!" they said.

Poof! A Christmas kiss brought me back.

"Let's hire the elves," said Mrs. Claus.

Elves were exactly what my workshop needed.

They became happy, hardworking helpers.

Now that the toys are made, we can all go on vacation! Cowabunga!